DISNEY'S

OLIVER
& Company

Based on Walt Disney's
full-length animated movie

Adapted by Jan Carr

Hippo

Scholastic Children's Books,
Commonwealth House, 1–19 New Oxford Street,
London WC1A 1NU, UK
a division of Scholastic Ltd

London ~ New York ~ Toronto ~ Sydney ~ Auckland

First published by Scholastic Inc., 1988
This edition published by Scholastic Ltd, 1997

Copyright © Disney, 1988

ISBN 0 590 19504 2

Typeset by Rowland Phototypesetting Ltd
Bury St Edmunds, Suffolk
Printed by Cox & Wyman, Reading, Berks

1

New York City is a very big city, one of the largest in the world. The buildings are tall and the streets are bustling. Lots of people live in New York, and it sometimes seems that they're all in a hurry. It's not an easy place to find a friend.

On one small corner of this great big city there was an old cardboard box. Inside the box were seven little kittens. Each of them was cute, and each of them was soft and cuddly. People hurried by. Would anyone stop to stroke the kittens? Maybe someone would even want to adopt one. Maybe someone loving would come along and give a kitten a nice, warm home.

The kittens pawed each other and scrambled to the edge of the box. One by one, passersby did stop. One by one, people found themselves opening up their hearts to one of the kittens and taking it home. The kittens meowed and purred. They climbed over each other. All of them were hungry and hoping for a home.

Day faded into night. The streets grew quiet. When darkness fell, all the kittens had been adopted except one, the little ginger-coloured one. This last little kitten didn't even have a name. Later, a little girl would give him one, a grand name, a stately name— Oliver. So that's what we'll call him now.

As Oliver waited alone in the dark, it started to rain. He huddled against the cardboard box, but big, wet drops soaked his fur. Rain flooded the box and washed Oliver out into the night streets. He would have to find shelter.

The little kitten stumbled down the street and turned into an alley. There, a pack of hungry dogs was scrounging through a rubbish bin for food.

"*Grrrr!*" they said when they saw Oliver. He looked enough like food to them! Oliver took off running, and the dogs chased right behind. He tore down the alley. He scrambled over a fence. Safety!

That night Oliver slept under the mudguard of an old, parked truck. He was on his own now. He was one tiny kitten in a big, scary world.

2

The next morning, Oliver woke up with a start. Someone was in the truck, starting the engine! The kitten hopped off the wheel and onto the street. All around him, New York was waking up. People were rushing down the pavements, hurrying off to work. Maybe one of them would be his friend.

"Hey!" came a voice. "Get your sausages here. Come and get it! Sausages!"

Food! When Oliver smelled the sweet, fatty sausages, he knew he was hungry. He sidled up to the sausage man and rubbed against his leg.

"Shoo! Get out of here!" the sausage man said.

The man kicked Oliver off his leg. He landed in a big pile of rubbish.

Across the alley sat a dog, a clever, streetwise canine. His name was Dodger and he was hungry for breakfast, too. He had been watching Oliver and the sausage man and he had an idea.

3

"Boy," he called to the small cat. "You sure picked the wrong guy to get hot dogs from."

Oliver backed away at the sight of the dog.

"Get away from me!" he hissed.

"Whoa, chill out, man!" said Dodger. "I don't eat cats. Too much fur." Dodger looked the kitten over.

"I've been watching you," he said, "and I think you're in need of some professional guidance. What do you say we team up and get some of those hot dogs?"

"Oh, no!" said Oliver. "I'm not going back there again."

"It'll be a snap, kid," said Dodger. "I'm an expert. All you've got to do is learn some moves."

"Moves?" asked Oliver.

"Yeah, you know, moves," said Dodger. "Tempo. Rhythm. This city's got a beat. Once you've got the beat, you can do anything."

"I can?" asked Oliver.

"Absitively. Posolutely," said Dodger.

The smell of the sausages filled the morning air. Oliver's stomach rumbled.

"So when do we get the food?" he asked.

Dodger looked over at the sausage cart. He grinned. Now!

"*RARARARAR!*" he growled suddenly.

Oliver jumped up and took off in fright. Dodger

laughed. This was exactly as he had planned. The dog chased the kitten right towards the cart. The terrified cat flew up at the sausage man and scrambled up on his chest.

"Ow! Ohhh! Get outta here!" shouted the man.

While the man was shouting, Dodger grabbed a long string of hot dogs from the cart and ran off. The kitten escaped right behind him and caught up with his new friend.

"Hey," said Dodger, when they were safe, "you've really got that rhythm, kid."

"We were good, huh!" said Oliver. "So when are we gonna eat?"

"We?" asked Dodger. "Ha, ha, ha! Listen, kid, I hate to break it to you, but our partnership is herewith dissolved."

"But you said. . ." said Oliver. "Hey, that's not fair."

"Fairs are for tourists, kid," said Dodger. "Check you later."

With that, Dodger twirled the string of hot dogs around his neck and started to trot off.

"Wait!" cried Oliver. "I helped you get those! Half of those are mine!"

The kitten ran after Dodger, but Dodger knew the streets and scampered ahead. The dog had his food now and he was heading home. He smiled and winked at the pretty female dogs who were out for their morning walks. He wove quickly through the tangled city traffic.

Oliver scrambled behind as best he could. He followed Dodger down the long streets and across the wide city. The kitten was still hungry and had nowhere else to go.

3

Oliver followed Dodger to the edge of the city. There, on the riverfront, was an old, rickety pier. Next to it was an abandoned barge. This was not the fancy part of town. The barge was filled with old, beaten-up furniture and broken-down appliances. Dodger lived there with a pack of other dogs. They called it home.

One of the dogs, Einstein, was an old, slow Great Dane. Another of them, Rita, was a pretty, long-haired Afghan hound. Tito, a tiny Chihuahua, was nosing through a pile of junk. Francis, a big, blubbery bulldog, was watching TV.

Tito pulled a badly chewed-up wallet out of the junk pile and carried it over to a box filled with loot.

"Hey, Frankie man," he said. "Watcha watching? Does he get the girl?"

"Shut up, you little rodent," said Francis. "I'm watching Shakespeare. And my name is Francis. Not Frankie. FRANCIS!"

"No kidding, man," said Tito. "So what'd you bring in today, FRAWN-CIS?"

Across the room, Einstein held up a broken tennis racquet. "Look what I've got," he said.

Tito snickered. "Man, what we need is some quality stuff. Check it out." He picked the wallet back up in his mouth and proudly showed it off.

It was Francis's turn to laugh. "Ooooh, shredded leather," he sneered.

"Shredded what?" said Tito. "What you talking about, man? That's not a cheap wallet!"

"Aw, cut it out, you two," said Rita. She looked over the ratty pieces of loot. "Fagin's not gonna be too happy with this stuff." She shook her head. "So, Francis," she sighed. "You've got the food, right?"

"Well," Francis paused. "No."

"Oh, Frankie!" The other three dogs all groaned.

"All you ever do is watch TV!" said Rita. "You knew it was your turn to get the food today!"

Francis shrugged. The dogs all began shouting. Then Dodger strolled through the door.

"Whoa, cool it, Dodger fans," he said. "I'd like to introduce you to your dinner. Hot dogs à la Dodger."

Dodger tossed the string of hot dogs to his friends. They all pounced on the food.

"All right, Dodger man!" said Tito with his mouth full. "You is El Maximo!"

8

"So how'd you do it this time, Dodgey baby?" asked Rita.

Dodger settled back to tell his story. Above him, on the roof of the barge, Oliver crouched low and watched the dogs through a jagged hole.

"What happened?" said Tito. "What happened? Didja haveta fight? How many were there?"

"It was tough," said Dodger. If they wanted a story, he would tell a good one. "Picture the city. The traffic's roaring and the hot dogs are sizzling. Enter Dodger, one cool puppy, community-minded. But he's not the only one out there. Enter the opposition—a greedy, ugly, psychotic monster with razor-sharp claws and dripping fangs."

Dodger's friends leaned in closer, listening to the story. On the roof, Oliver leaned in closer, too. Razor-sharp claws? Dripping fangs? Was Dodger talking about *him*?

"He comes at me, eyes burning," said Dodger. "I knew my time had come." Dodger's eyes narrowed. "Suddenly. . ." he continued.

But Dodger never got to finish his story. CRASH! Oliver fell through the hole in the roof and into a line of laundry stretched across the barge. His legs got tangled up in the clothes. KA-PLUNK! He landed in the middle of the gang.

"Watch out!" cried Tito. "Gang war!"

The dogs ran behind the furniture for cover.

"What is it?" said Rita, peering out.

Tito stepped up to the wriggling ball of laundry. The frightened kitten dug his claws into the clothing and ripped his way out.

"Ay!" screamed Tito. "It's an alien!"

Rita walked closer and took a better look.

"Cool it, guys," she laughed. "It's just a cat."

4

Oliver crouched in fear. The dogs walked over to take a look. What was a cat doing on their barge? All the dogs were curious. All but Dodger, who knew just what that kitten was doing on the barge. Dodger slunk over to an armchair. He turned on the TV. He slid low in the chair, hoping his story wouldn't be found out.

"How'd you find this place, cat?" asked Rita.

"I . . . I . . . followed this dog," said Oliver.

"Why would a cat follow a dog?" asked Francis.

"I just want some of the sausages I helped him get," said the kitten.

Tito didn't believe him. "He's lying!" he shouted. "He's a spy, man. Let's eat him. You're dead meat, kitty!"

"I . . . I saw him come down here," said Oliver. He looked around the room. He spotted Dodger. "Hey," he said. "That's him over there!"

Dodger tried to stay cool.

"Hey, kitty," he said, a little too casually. "What took you so long?"

Rita looked at Francis. Francis looked at Rita. The game was up. Dodger had been caught in his lie.

"Dripping fangs, indeed," said Francis.

"I like the burning eyes!" laughed Rita.

Dodger squirmed. "Hey, keep it down, guys," he said. "The game's on."

Tito poked playfully at Dodger. "Come on, man," he said. "Let's see this big, bad kitty-fighter in action." He jabbed at Dodger again. "*Grrr*," he growled. It was a challenge.

Dodger jumped on Tito. Francis joined in the brawl.

"Oh, boy, a dog pile!" said Einstein. He jumped in, too. Soon all the dogs were in a wild, snapping snarl. Oliver leaped away and jumped in the box of loot for safety.

The door burst open and a man walked in. He was wearing ragged clothes, and a coat that was much too big. In his hands he held a battered box of dog biscuits. This was Fagin, the dogs' master.

"All right!" he yelled. "Knock it off! Come on! Knock it off!"

The dogs slid apart guiltily.

"What's the matter with you guys?" Fagin scolded. "Don't you understand? Sykes will be here any minute."

The dogs looked at Fagin. They spied the box of dog biscuits. *Ruff!* They jumped up on their master, barking and wagging their tails. They licked him, tickling him with their tongues. Oliver peered out from inside the loot box and watched.

"All right," Fagin giggled. "Settle down."

Honk! Honk! Fagin froze at the sound. A car pulled up outside.

"Oh, no!" he said. "It's Sykes! All right, all right," he called. "I'm coming!"

Einstein nosed the loot box across the floor to his master. Fagin picked it up and tore through it in disbelief.

"It's worthless," he cried. "What have you done?" His voice was trembling.

The little kitten poked his head up out of the loot.

"A pussycat?" Fagin groaned. "How are we ever going to pay Sykes off with a pussycat?"

Before Fagin could think of a plan, two Doberman pinschers burst through the door. They were snarling and growling. These Dobermans were Roscoe and DeSoto, two very vicious dogs. They'd been sent by Sykes.

"Oh," said Fagin, trying to sound calm. "Look who's here, kids. Company."

Oliver jumped out of the loot box and hid behind the legs of an ironing board.

"Nice doggies," said Fagin. He hugged the loot to

himself. The Dobermans growled as he inched out the door.

Fagin climbed up the pier and walked up to the long, shiny black car apprehensively. Inside the car was the dreaded Sykes.

"Mr Sykes," said Fagin. "Hello. Lovely evening. Ha ha."

He squeezed into the narrow space between the car and the end of the pier. The driver's window was closed. Fagin chattered on nervously.

"In fact," he said, "I was just saying that very thing to your two, lovely pure-bred Dobermans."

The window slid down. Sykes grabbed the box from Fagin's hands.

"The money, Fagin," he said.

"Actually," Fagin stuttered, "I've got something much better than money. Some luxury items."

Sykes rifled through the box. A shredded wallet, a broken hair dryer, nothing but rubbish. He shoved the box back at Fagin.

"I don't want your junk, Fagin," he said.

Sykes opened the car door, knocking Fagin to the edge of the high pier. He emptied his ashtray on Fagin's shoes.

"I don't think you grasp the severity of the situation," he said.

Fagin grabbed the side mirror of the car and held on for dear life. He teetered at the edge of the pier.

Sykes reached out the window and grabbed him tightly by the collar.

"Mr Fagin," Sykes hissed. "I lent you money and I want it back. Do you know what happens when I don't see my money?"

Sykes blew a plume of cigar smoke in Fagin's face. Fagin choked and gulped for air.

"People get hurt," said Sykes. "People like you." He pulled tighter on Fagin's collar. "Do I make myself clear?" he sneered.

5

Back inside the barge, Oliver crouched, watching the Dobermans. One, DeSoto, had caught a cat's scent and was circling his hiding place, sniffing the floor. The other, Roscoe, was leering at Rita.

"You know," he snorted, "I can't work out why you want to hang around a dump like this when you could be living uptown with a class act like myself."

Tiny, wiry Tito jumped forward.

"Come on, man," he said to the big Doberman. "You guys don't scare me. I'll fight you both, man."

Old Einstein put one of his big paws on Tito to hold him back.

"Why don't you pick on someone your own size?" Einstein said to Roscoe.

"Like you, old man?" Roscoe laughed.

Roscoe wanted a fight. He turned and knocked the TV set off its crate. Glass shattered across the room. Roscoe looked at the gang and smiled a slow, menacing smile.

Out on the pier, Fagin was also in trouble. He was kneeling at the side of the car, begging Sykes for mercy.

"Oh, please! Oh, please! Oh, please!" Fagin whimpered.

Sykes held up three fingers. "I'll give you three sunrises. Three sunsets. Three days, Fagin," he said.

"Three, three, three." Fagin added the numbers quickly in his head. "Nine?" he asked hopefully.

"No, Fagin!" screamed Sykes. "Three!"

Sykes rolled the car window shut. The matter was closed. Fagin crumpled at the edge of the dock.

"Just three days?" he cried. "Only three days?"

Sykes beeped the car horn loudly. Fagin lost his balance and toppled from the edge of the pier into the cold, rolling waters below.

Inside, the Dobermans heard the horn. Roscoe turned to go, but DeSoto reached his paw under the legs of the ironing board. He'd found what he'd been looking for, a frightened little kitten.

"Hey, Roscoe, look what I found," said DeSoto.

Honk! Honk! Sykes was calling them to the car.

"Forget it, DeSoto," said Roscoe. "We gotta go."

DeSoto slid closer to Oliver. He licked his lips. His eyes glinted.

"I like cats," he said. "I like to eat them."

DeSoto lunged at the tiny cat. Oliver swiped his bared claw across DeSoto's nose.

17

"*YEEOW!*" yelled DeSoto. He leaped away, wiping blood from his nose.

Roscoe started angrily for Oliver, but Dodger jumped between them and growled.

"That's enough, Roscoe," he said.

Honk! HOOOONK!

Rita moved in to back up Dodger. "Run along, Roscoe," she said. "Your master's calling."

Roscoe backed off, but he was still growling.

"We ain't finished yet, Dodger," he said. Roscoe and DeSoto edged their way out the door. "You guys are going to pay for this," said Roscoe. "Starting with that cat."

6

All of the dogs in the gang gathered around Oliver. They were very impressed. He was only a little cat, but he'd taken on the Dobermans. And won!

"All right!" said Tito. "Those creeps will think twice before hassling us again, man."

Dodger looked at Oliver proudly.

"What'd I tell you, guys?" he said. "Old Dodge can really pick 'em, huh?"

Across the barge the door banged open. A very wet Fagin plodded heavily across the room.

"Three days," he whimpered. "How am I ever going to come up with all that money?"

Fagin collapsed into a chair.

"What's the use?" he said. "I'll never get out from under that maniac. My days are numbered and the number is three."

Poor Fagin. All the dogs ran over and snuggled up to him. They hated to see their master so upset. Dodger slipped off Fagin's shoes while Tito fetched his slippers. Einstein picked a dog biscuit up off the floor and nudged it into Fagin's hand. Fagin nibbled at it absently.

"Thanks, guys," he said.

Einstein licked Fagin's face. Fagin began to smile.

"Hey, that reminds me," Fagin said, suddenly. "I saw DeSoto's nose. Who did that?"

Dodger nudged Oliver forward through the gang. Fagin scooped the little cat up in his arms.

"You!" Fagin laughed. "That took a lot of guts." Fagin rubbed the fur under Oliver's chin. "We've never had a cat in the gang before. We can use all the help we can get."

Oliver's heart beat faster. Could he really be part of the gang? Had he really found a home?

Fagin leaned back in his chair and yawned widely. It had been a long and tiring day.

"All right," he said. "Time for bed. We've got a big day tomorrow."

Einstein nuzzled up to Fagin's side. The dog was holding a book in his mouth.

"*Mmm*," he whimpered. "*Mmm mmm*." He wanted Fagin to read.

"Oh, all right," said Fagin. "But just one chapter tonight."

All the dogs circled around. They loved it when Fagin read them their bedtime story.

This story was their favourite. It was about a dog

named Sparky. Sparky lived in the country. He rolled in green fields and played with wild rabbits.

Oliver nestled in Fagin's lap and listened to the lulling story. The dogs lay down at Fagin's feet and began to drift off to sleep. Dodger stood up and stretched. He moved sleepily across the room and settled himself under his own blanket. Oliver hopped off Fagin's lap and scampered over to his friend's bed. He lay down at Dodger's side and snuggled into the dog's soft fur.

Dodger and his new friend fell asleep together, warm and cosy.

As Fagin read on about Sparky and the clean country air, night settled over this old city barge and its unusual family.

7

The next morning the gang was up early, ready for work. They had a lot of money to bring in and only three days to get it.

Fagin loaded the gang into the back of his motorized trike and spluttered off into the traffic.

"Well, gang," he called back to the animals. "This is the big one. We've got three days to do or die."

Fagin veered the trike through traffic, passing cars and honking his horn.

"Dodger," he instructed, "you keep an eye on the new kid, show him the ropes. And listen," he said, "I don't want to put any undue pressure on you, but as you march off to duty, I want you to keep one thing in mind. DEAD MEN DO NOT BUY DOG FOOD!"

Fagin steered the trike into an alley and lurched to a stop. The dogs piled out of the trike. Fagin called out their last instructions.

"So, big smiles," he shouted. "Get out there and FETCH!"

Fagin had let the gang out on Columbus Avenue, a street lined with fancy shops. The things in the shops were expensive. The people who shopped there had lots of money.

"All right," said Dodger. "If Mr Sykes doesn't see some cold hard cash soon, we are Doberman nosh. Come on."

He led the gang across the street and down the pavement. Oliver trotted along. He was anxious to get started.

"What do we do, anyway?" he asked.

Tito snickered.

"Investment banking, man," said Tito. "Don't you read about us in *The Wall Street Journal*?"

Oliver shook his head. "No," he said, innocently.

"We're captains of industry," said Francis.

"Oh," said Oliver. That sounded good to him. "Can I be one, too?"

"Sure, kid," said Dodger. "Now pay attention and learn."

Dodger looked down the street. If the gang needed money, he would figure out a way to get it. As luck would have it, a long, gleaming black limousine turned the corner and cruised right towards the gang. Perfect! This was just what Dodger needed. He knew exactly what to do.

23

"All right!" said Dodger. "A chauffeur shuffle!"

The gang gathered in a huddle around him. Dodger laid out the plan.

"Einstein, give me a bumper bender," he said. "Tito, you're in charge of electronics. Rita and I will work the crowd. Francis—"

"I know," Francis smiled. "My public awaits."

"What about me?" asked Oliver. "What do I do?"

"You help Tito," said Dodger.

"Come on, cat," said Tito. "Uncle Tito will show you how it's done."

Tito ran after the limousine, and the kitten followed close behind. The two of them leaped onto the back bumper of the car.

"Ready, go!" Dodger called to the others.

Inside the limousine, a little girl was riding with her chauffeur. The little girl had chestnut hair and wide blue eyes. Her name was Jenny. She was reading a letter she had just received from her parents.

"Oh, Winston," she said to the chauffeur. "Listen to this." She read the letter out loud. "After a little sightseeing we left Paris by car for the con . . . fer . . . ence. . ."

"Conference," said Winston, helping her along.

"Oh, yes, conference," said Jenny. She continued reading, "in Rome on Wednesday." Her face fell as she read more. "Jenny, I'm afraid your father and I won't be able to make it. . ."

As he drove along, Winston looked at the little girl in his rear view mirror.

"Is there anything wrong, Jenny?" he asked. Her voice had trailed off and had sounded so sad. "Are your parents all right?"

"They're staying longer," Jenny said glumly.

"Oh, don't worry," Winston said, trying to cheer her. "They'll be home for your birthday."

"I don't think so," said Jenny. She stared out the window and heaved a great sigh.

As the limousine rounded a corner, Einstein leaped out at the car and banged into its side with all his might. The limo screeched to a halt.

"What was that?" asked Jenny.

"I don't know," said Winston. "But don't be alarmed. I'll be right back."

Outside the car, Einstein reeled from the crash. Francis hustled him away and then took his place. The big, hammy bulldog lay down in front of the limo. He angled himself right in front of its heavy front wheels.

8

When Winston stepped out of the limousine to see what had happened, Tito and Oliver hopped off the back bumper and scrambled into the car.

"Hey, check it out, man," said Tito. He grabbed the steering wheel and gave it a whirl. "Forget Fagin, man. Let's take this baby to Atlantic City."

But Tito had work to do. His job was to disconnect the car stereo and make off with it. He hopped off the seat and got to work, gnawing the wires with his teeth.

"Hey, Tito, what can I do?" asked Oliver.

"Why don't you be a lookout?" Tito mumbled. "Look out the window and make sure it's still daylight."

Outside the car, Winston had stooped over Francis. Francis was moaning and howling, as if he were in pain, as if he had been hit head-on by the limousine.

"Oh, what have I done?" Winston cried. "Poor thing."

Around them a crowd had gathered. People were sure that Francis was hurt.

"I . . . I'm sure he's all right," Winston stuttered.

Francis howled louder. The people pressed closer. Dodger and Rita slipped in and out of the crowd, picking pockets and snatching purses.

"What's Dodge doing?" Oliver asked innocently, as he looked out the window.

"Quiet, man," said Tito. "This is a delicate operation."

Suddenly, from behind Oliver came a whirring sound. He spun around. Someone was buzzing down the window that separated the back of the car from the front.

"Hey, Tito," said Oliver. "There's something back there."

Tito was too busy to pay even a bit of attention to the kitten. Oliver stared dumbly at the little girl in the back seat of the car. He backed up in fear and slipped off the edge of the dashboard. His foot slipped into the ring of the ignition key. The key turned. The car started. Electricity surged through Tito.

"*Yeow!*" Tito shot out of the car.

"Let's get out of here!" shouted Dodger.

Francis jumped up from Winston's arms and took off running. The rest of the gang dropped everything and ran right behind.

"What's going on here?" said Winston. He rushed

back to the car. "Jenny," he asked, "are you all right?"

Jenny had picked the kitten up and was cradling him in her arms.

"Poor little kitty," she crooned. "Let me help you."

Down the block, the gang was hiding in an alley. They were panting and looking around nervously.

"Where's the kid?" asked Rita.

"He must still be in the car, man," said Tito.

The gang peered out to the street. The limousine was pulling out. There was the kitten in the back window. His eyes were wide and frightened.

"Oh, that poor little guy," said Rita. "What are we going to do, Dodge?"

"Tito," said Dodge, "you come with me. The rest of you go back to Fagin."

Dodger and Tito ran off into traffic. They chased the limousine across town, to a posh, very rich neighbourhood.

Winston pulled up in front of an elegant sandstone home. Jenny got out of the car. She was still holding the kitten.

"Now *really*, Jenny," said Winston. "We can't just take in a stray off the street."

"But look at the poor thing," said Jenny.

"I know you're growing attached to him," said

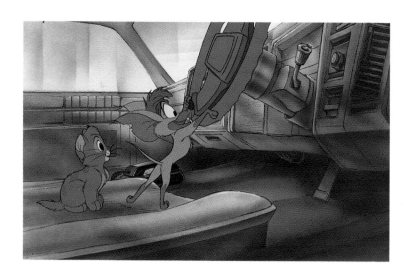

Winston, "but your parents left me responsible for you."

"They won't mind," said Jenny. She gave the kitten's forehead a soft, sweet kiss. "Don't worry, kitty," she said. "I'll take care of you."

Winston followed Jenny up the stairs and into the house. He shook his head. He clicked his tongue.

"Georgette is not going to like this," he said.

9

Winston headed up the long flight of stairs that led to the first floor of the house. He opened one of the bedroom doors. He turned on the light.

"Rise and shine, Georgette," he said. "The world anxiously awaits your arrival."

Winston was talking to a fluffy lavender poodle who still lay lazily in bed. The poodle stretched. She yawned. She stumbled out of bed and sat down at her dressing table.

"Oooh," she said, as she looked at herself in the mirror. "We've got some work to do."

Georgette pulled the curlers from her hair and powdered her face. She sprayed perfume behind her ears. She was, indeed, a fancy-looking dog. Her room was filled with ribbons and trophies she had won at dog shows.

"Oh, look at me," Georgette smiled, very pleased with her work. "I am one pretty pup."

All the neighbourhood male dogs thought so, too. Georgette threw open her curtains and stepped out onto her terrace. In the garden below, male dogs came running from every direction. Georgette tossed them a smile and then whirled back inside. She was ready to start her day.

Downstairs, in the kitchen, Jenny was bustling around, getting breakfast for her kitten. She cooked some eggs. She mixed in some cereal and spooned a big dollop of sour cream on top.

"I bet you're starving, huh?" she asked the cat. "Wait till you taste this. It's a secret recipe I just invented."

The kitten cowered between the legs of a kitchen stool.

"Don't be scared, silly," said Jenny. "This is your home now."

Jenny poured the breakfast mixture into a pink china bowl. The bowl was labelled "Georgette." Winston walked into the kitchen and halted as he saw the big mess.

"My goodness, Jenny," he said, "don't you think a tin of kitty chow would have sufficed?"

"Nonsense," said Jenny. "He'll love this." Then she looked thoughtful. "I think I'll call him Oliver."

Winston was about to lecture her when the phone rang. He bustled out to the hall to answer it.

"Jenny," he called. "It's your parents."

"Wait till I tell them about Oliver," Jenny cried. "They're going to be so excited."

Jenny set Oliver's breakfast down and ran for the phone. Georgette paraded past her and into the kitchen. The poodle stopped short when she got to the door. Could she believe her eyes? What in the world was that she saw? A *cat*? Eating out of *her* bowl?

Georgette walked over to Oliver. She smiled a fake-sweet smile.

"Hello," she said. "Do you happen to know whose bowl you're eating out of?"

"Yours?" gulped Oliver.

"Oooh. Aren't you a clever kitty?" said Georgette. "And do you have any idea whose home this is?"

"I thought it was J-J-Jenny's," said Oliver.

"It may be Jenny's house," said Georgette, "but everything from the doorknobs down is MINE!"

Georgette moved towards Oliver and opened her mouth wide. She was just about to bite into the little kitten when Jenny walked back in the kitchen.

"Oh, Georgette," said Jenny. "I see you've met Oliver. Isn't he cute? I've got great news. Mum and Dad just said I could keep him." Jenny patted Georgette on the head. "I'm sure you two are going to be the best of friends."

Georgette broke into a sick, leering smile. Georgette wanted Oliver out. And Georgette *always* got her way.

10

At first, Oliver was a little shy in his new home, but he soon warmed up. From the start, Jenny cared for him so much. She made him feel welcome. She made him feel loved. That morning, after breakfast, Jenny sat down to practise her piano.

"I've got to practise now, kitty," she said.

As Jenny started her scales, Oliver hopped onto the keyboard and walked across it. Jenny laughed. She stroked Oliver's fur. As she played, she made up a special song about how much she loved her new little kitten.

After she finished practising, Jenny took Oliver all around New York. They went rowing in Central Park. They ate ice-cream and took a carriage ride. Then Jenny took Oliver to a fancy jewellery shop. She bought him his very own collar with a gold pendant dangling from it. The pendant was engraved. It read, "Oliver. 1125 Fifth Avenue."

Oliver was really Jenny's pet now. He loved Jenny

and he loved his new home. That night Oliver slept next to Jenny, cuddled on her bed.

"Good night, Oliver," Jenny whispered in his ear.

Winston peeked in on the two sleeping friends. He tucked the blankets around them and turned out the light.

11

The next morning was a school day. Jenny grabbed her books and ran out to the school bus.

"Goodbye, Winston. Goodbye, Oliver," she called.

As the bus drove off, Dodger and the gang stepped out into the open. They'd been hiding across the street, behind some bushes. They had come to save Oliver. They crept up to the house.

This was a rescue mission and each dog in the gang knew exactly what to do. Einstein, the tallest, reached up and rang the front bell with his nose. Francis planted himself on the pavement. He lay down and writhed in fake pain.

"You!!!" cried Winston, when he opened the door. "I'll show you, you. . ."

Winston grabbed a broom and chased after Francis. Once Winston was out the door, the rest of the gang slipped in and slammed the door behind them. Even Francis skittered through. Winston was left outside, still looking for Francis.

The gang had got into the house! They looked up at the tall, grand entrance.

"Wow!" said Tito. "Check this place out!"

The house was indeed rich, richer than anything the gang had ever seen. The floors were covered with luxurious carpets. The walls were filled with magnificent paintings. Rita looked around in awe.

"This place looks pretty nice, Dodger," she said. "How bad off could the cat be here?"

"Really, man," said Tito. "If this is torture, chain me to the wall."

Behind them, the door rattled. Winston was back.

"All right, enough," whispered Dodger. "We came to get the kid."

The gang snuck up the stairs to look for their friend. They tried a door. Inside, they didn't find Oliver—they found Georgette.

Georgette was at her dressing table, putting on perfume. She was still upset about Oliver and Jenny.

"I love you, Oliver," she hissed, imitating Jenny. "Play with Georgette." How could Jenny have said that? "I'd like to play with that cat all right," Georgette went on. "The little fur ball."

Dodger opened the bedroom door.

"*AAAGGHH!*" Georgette screamed. Who was

36

this intruder? What did he want? Georgette barked and backed into the mirror.

"Don't come any closer!" she screamed. "Do you know who I am?" She pointed to all her ribbons and trophies. "Six-time national champion!"

Dodger laughed. "We're all impressed, right, guys?" he said.

The gang gathered around Georgette. She looked them up and down. They're mutts, she thought, all of them. Tito was staring at her trophies.

"*Very* impressed," he said huskily. He wagged his tail. His heart was pounding. He'd never met such an important dog before. He took Georgette's paw.

"Allow me to introduce myself," he said.

"Get away from me, you little bug-eyed creep!" Georgette screamed.

The other dogs walked around the room. Francis lay down on the bed and opened a tin of dog biscuits. Rita looked at Georgette's photographs. Einstein sniffed at Georgette's dressing table and stuck his nose into her powder.

"*Ah choo!*" he sneezed.

Downstairs, Winston heard the noise.

"All right, that does it," said Georgette. "You yo-yos clear out, and I mean now!"

"Relax, champ," said Dodger. "We'll leave as soon as we get our cat."

Cat? Did he say cat? This was Georgette's big chance, her chance to get rid of Oliver.

"Your cat?" Georgette smiled. "How stupid of me. You must be the friends he keeps talking about."

Winston was coming up the stairs. Georgette had to act fast. She hustled the gang into Jenny's bedroom. Oliver was asleep in the middle of Jenny's pillow. On his face was a sweet smile. He certainly looked comfortable. He certainly looked at home.

"Oh, Dodger," said Rita. "Look at him. Maybe we'd better forget the whole thing."

Georgette picked Oliver up by the collar and threw him into a pillowcase.

"Here, now get going!" she said. "Hurry! Use the fire escape!"

The gang slipped out the window. Tito stayed behind.

"No time for long goodbyes, baby," he said to Georgette, "but here's something to remember me by."

Tito leaned forward to kiss Georgette on the lips.

SLAP! Georgette knocked him out the window, and Tito fell down the fire escape.

His friends ran to him, but Tito wasn't hurt. He was even grinning.

"I think she likes me, man!" he said.

12

When they got back to the barge, Einstein shook Oliver out of the bag.

"What's going on?" Oliver blinked.

"Just the rescue of the century, man," said Tito.

"Rescue?" said Oliver. "But—"

"You should've seen Tito handle Miss Six-time National Champion," Dodger laughed.

Rita looked at Oliver. She was still worried.

"You OK, kid?" she asked.

"I'm fine," said Oliver, "but I was happy there. Why did you guys take me?"

The gang members looked at him, confused.

"We rescued you, kitty," said Einstein. "We brought you home."

"But I have another home now," said Oliver, "and someone who loves me."

"What do you mean, kid?" said Dodger. "You're in the gang."

Dodger's feelings were hurt. Oliver was *his* friend,

part of *his* family. "I'm sorry," said Oliver, "but all I ever wanted was—"

Dodger cut him off.

"What, this place not good enough for you any more? Don't want to mix with the riffraff?"

"No, I . . . I like you," said Oliver. "I like every one of you. But there was a little girl . . . I just want to go back."

Rita shook her head. "We never should have taken him, Dodge," she said. "We were wrong."

So, Dodger thought, the cat has a new home now. He doesn't even care about the gang.

"You want to leave?" Dodger said to Oliver. "Fine. There's the door."

Oliver hung his head. He hadn't meant to hurt his friends, but he did want to go back to his real home.

"Go on," said Dodger. "No one's stopping you."

Oliver walked sadly out the door. He started up the stairs. As he was going up, Fagin was coming down. Fagin was worried about Sykes. He scooped Oliver up in his arms.

"I've got two hours," Fagin murmured. "How can I ever pay off Sykes?"

Fagin carried Oliver over to his chair and slumped down. Fagin was whimpering. He stroked Oliver's head. His hand ran over Oliver's new gold collar.

"Hey, what's this?" said Fagin. He read the printed tag. "Oliver. 1125 Fifth Avenue."

"So that's where you've been," Fagin chuckled. "Your owner probably spends more on catnip than we do on food in a month. He's probably worried. Only his money to comfort him. Only his millions and millions. . ."

Millions? Fagin brightened. That gave him an idea. A big idea. He started giggling. He started laughing. He couldn't stop. The gang stared at him. They'd never seen their master quite like this. Fagin grabbed a piece of paper. He grabbed a crayon. He started to write a ransom note. He had decided to ransom Oliver for money.

Dear Mr Rich, he wrote. *Mr Very Rich. . .*

13

After he sent the ransom note, Fagin stuck Oliver in his pocket and went to talk to Sykes. Sykes's office was in an old warehouse. The warehouse yard was cluttered and dark. It was filled with rusty girders and broken-down cranes. It was not very inviting.

Fagin stood outside the door, practising what he would say to Sykes. He'd brought Dodger with him, too. Dodger listened and nodded his head.

"It's a watertight plan, Sykes," said Fagin. "Simple and sweet. I ransom the kitty and you get paid in full tomorrow. It's my final offer. Take it or leave it."

It sounded good to Dodger. Fagin took a deep breath and pressed the buzzer at the door.

"Yeah, who is it?" Sykes's voice boomed over the speaker.

"Uhhhh. . ." Suddenly Fagin was so frightened, he couldn't even say his name.

Sykes buzzed them in.

Inside the office, Sykes sat at his big desk. Roscoe and DeSoto were there, too. They bared their teeth. Sykes was on the phone.

"Right." He gave instructions to someone on the other end. "You know what happens to clients who don't pay their debts on time. Start with the knuckles. Then the cement shoes. No, don't kill him . . . yet."

Sykes hung up the phone.

"So, Fagin," he smiled. "Did you bring me something green and wrinkly to make me happy?"

"Sykes," said Fagin. His voice was small. "I have a watertight kitty. I mean plan, plan."

"What about the money, Fagin?" Sykes's smile hardened into a dark scowl.

Fagin tried to explain about his plan. He pulled Oliver out of his pocket. "I got this kitty," he said. "See?" Fagin was having trouble explaining his plan. Sykes was making him nervous. And so were those two Dobermans.

The Dobermans circled Fagin. Their lips curled and their eyes glinted.

"Fagin!" Sykes's voice boomed. "You don't have the money!"

Sykes snapped his fingers and the Dobermans leaped to attack Fagin.

"NO, STOP!" cried Fagin. "STOP, SYKES! PLEASE!"

Dodger leaped up at the Dobermans and fought

them back. The two vicious dogs knocked him down and bit at him. They tumbled across the floor.

"Please, Sykes!" Fagin cried. "I'm getting your money. It's coming tonight! It's from a rich cat. I mean, from a rich family."

Fagin rushed over to Sykes and thrust little Oliver at him.

"They're coming tonight," he cried. "With the money I owe you. To get the cat back!"

Sykes took a look at the little kitten. He snapped his fingers a second time. The Dobermans backed off. Dodger fell wounded to the floor.

Sykes fingered Oliver's collar and rubbed the gold tag between his fingers.

"Hmmm. Fifth Avenue," he said. "I'm proud of you, Fagin. You're starting to think big."

Fagin lifted Dodger in his arms. Oliver jumped quickly to join them. The three trudged back out the door, into the dark night.

"You've got twelve hours," Sykes called after them. "And Fagin! This is your last chance!"

14

When Jenny received the ransom note, she knew she had to rescue her kitten. So she set out that night, accompanied by Georgette.

Jenny led Georgette through the dirty, dimly lit streets. It seemed as if they'd been walking for ever and getting nowhere. Jenny stopped and unfolded Fagin's letter. She studied the map he had drawn.

"Oh, Georgette," she said. "I can't read this."

Jenny's eyes filled with tears. She looked to the left, then to the right. Neither way looked right. How would she ever find Oliver?

"Oh, Georgette," she cried. "We're lost!"

Fagin stood outside the barge, pacing back and forth. Where was Oliver's rich owner? He should be here by now. Fagin was worried. It was getting late.

"Where is he?" said Fagin. "What if he doesn't come? But wait. What if he does come and he's bigger than me? What if he's got a gun?"

The gang hid on the pier behind some crates. Jenny

came around the corner, pulling Georgette. Somewhere there had to be someone who could help her. Jenny spied Fagin. Maybe he could help.

"Excuse me, sir," she said.

Fagin jumped in fright.

"Oh!" he cried. "Please don't arrest me! Please! I..."

Then Fagin saw it was only a little girl. She looked tired. She looked afraid.

"Listen, little girl," he said, "you scared me half to death. You shouldn't be down here. This is a tough neighbourhood. You'd better go home."

"I can't," Jenny cried. "I'm lost."

"What are you doing down here, anyway?" Fagin asked her.

"I came to find my kitty," Jenny sobbed.

"YOUR KITTY!" Fagin choked. Was she talking about Oliver? This wasn't the rich master he expected. This was just a little girl.

"Somebody stole him," said Jenny. "They sent me this note."

Jenny held up the letter, the very one Fagin had written.

"Ohhh," Fagin groaned.

Jenny pulled a piggy bank out from under her coat.

"I even brought this to get him back," she said. "It's all I have."

"A piggy bank? That's awful," Fagin gulped.

"I know," said Jenny. "What kind of person would steal a poor little kitty?"

What in the world would Fagin do now? His plan had failed. Instead of a rich master, he had a little girl. Instead of a bagful of money, he had a child's piggy bank. And to make it worse, the little girl was so upset. She was crying. She missed her kitty. Fagin swallowed hard.

"Guess what," he said. "I found a little lost kitten. Take a look. Maybe he's yours."

Fagin lifted Oliver out of his pocket.

"Oliver!" cried Jenny.

Fagin handed the kitten over. Oliver mewed happily and licked Jenny's face. The two were reunited, but not for long. Across the pier, a car turned the corner. It sped right towards Jenny. It was Sykes. He zoomed past, opened the car door, and grabbed Jenny by the waist. Oliver fell to the ground. Sykes threw Jenny into the back of the car.

"Wait!" cried Fagin. "Stop! What are you doing?"

Sykes slammed the door and laughed.

"Keep your mouth shut, Fagin," he said. "And we'll consider our debt closed."

Sykes revved the engine and sped off as fast as he had come. The gang stood frozen on the pier.

"What happened?" cried Oliver. "Jenny! They took Jenny!"

"Don't worry," said Dodger. "We'll get her back!"

"You will?" asked Oliver, hopefully.

Dodger winked at him. "Absitively. Posolutely."

"Yeah, come on, man!" said Tito. "What are we waiting for?"

Georgette and the gang were off and running, chasing after Sykes. Fagin hopped on his trike.

"Wait!" he cried. "Wait for me!"

15

When the gang got to Sykes's warehouse, they crouched outside his door. Inside the warehouse, Sykes had Jenny tied to a chair.

"Don't cry, little girl," he scowled. "This is just a business arrangement between your family and me."

The gang pushed against the door. The place was locked up tight.

"Oh, man," said Tito. "It don't look good."

Dodger looked around. There must be some way. He spotted something in the pile of rubbish. It gave him an idea.

"Francis," he said. "Remember that old circus stunt you used to do?"

Dodger set a plank on top of a barrel. He tucked Oliver into an old football helmet and placed him down at one end of the board.

"Francis," he asked, "you all set?"

Francis nodded. The big, heavy dog jumped down onto the other end of the plank and the helmet went flying. It crashed through a window and bounced down inside. Oliver was in the warehouse. Quickly he scurried to a window on the first floor, unlatched it, and let the dogs in. Carefully, quietly, they crept through the dark halls. The Dobermans had heard them. They didn't have much time.

Deep in the warehouse, Sykes was at his desk. He checked the monitors behind him. The warehouse looked secure. He picked up the phone and called someone who owed him a favour.

"Give me a number for 1125 Fifth Avenue." Sykes was going to ransom Jenny, not Oliver.

At that moment, if Sykes had turned to check the monitors, he would've seen the gang creeping down the hall. The cameras were on them. They were being watched.

"Freeze!" said Dodger. He had spotted the camera. It was at the end of the hall.

"Yo, Tito," he whispered. If anyone could unhook the camera, Tito could.

"Right," Tito whispered back. "I'll check it out." He climbed up to the camera and began to chew on the wires. One by one, Sykes's monitors went black. The rest of the gang crept ahead. They piled up outside Sykes's office and knocked on the door.

Sykes threw a quick look at Jenny.

"Keep your trap shut," he said. "Don't make a sound."

When he opened the door, there was no one there. He walked out into the hall to investigate. The gang slipped into his office. They locked the door behind them.

Rita and Dodger ran right to Jenny and gnawed off the ropes that bound her hands. Oliver leaped up into Jenny's lap.

"Oh, Oliver!" Jenny cried.

Jenny held the soft kitten up to her cheek. The gang had found her! Was she saved?

16

Out in the hall, Sykes had worked out that something was wrong. He whistled for his Dobermans. They came running. He tried his office door. It was locked.

The gang started at the sound of the door. Sykes was back! They were trapped, with no way to escape!

"Oh, great!" cried Georgette. "We're going to die!"

Dodger looked up. Above them was a hook, hanging from the ceiling. It was rigged to an electric wire.

"Tito," said Dodger. "Hot-wiring time!"

Tito leaped on the backs of the gang and climbed up to the hook. He worked fast. Sykes was banging at the door. Tito connected some wires and lowered the hook down to the gang. They rigged the hook onto a chair and all jumped on.

BANG! Sykes knocked the door down. The Dobermans threw themselves at the chair, but Tito raised it higher, up beyond their reach.

Sykes ran for the control box that operated the hook. With one swoop of an axe, he smashed the controls. The system exploded. The chair, with the gang on it, crashed down onto the floor.

"HELP!" screamed Jenny.

There was only one other way to escape: the loading door. The gang ran for the door and Einstein pulled the chain that opened it. They were almost safe! They had almost escaped! Einstein gave the chain one last tug. There, outside the door, was Sykes. He had slipped around and was waiting for them. And so were his two Dobermans.

"Heh, heh, heh," Sykes laughed. "This has all been very entertaining, but the party is over."

The Dobermans poised for the attack, waiting for Sykes to snap his fingers. Suddenly, though, they were startled by a noise, an engine, a sputtering old motor. It was Fagin! On the trike! He raced into the warehouse and screeched into the middle of the gang.

"Come on!" he yelled. "Come on!"

Jenny, Oliver, Georgette and the gang hopped onto the back of the trike. Fagin accelerated and drove right past Sykes. The Dobermans leaped out of the way.

"Fagin!" Sykes screamed after him.

Fagin and the gang sped away. Sykes jumped in his car and tore after them.

Fagin looked in his rear view mirror. Sykes's

headlights glared behind him. Sykes was gaining fast. Fagin knew that his trike would never keep ahead. He knew he had to do something quickly.

17

Ahead of Fagin was an underground entrance. There was nowhere else to turn. Fagin drove his trike right down the underground stairs and dropped from sight.

Sykes screeched to a halt. He skidded his car down the stairs after Fagin and raced across the platform. Fagin drove his trike down onto the train tracks. Sykes followed. He raced his motor and zoomed towards Fagin.

"Come on!" Fagin shouted at his trike. "Faster! Faster!"

CRASH! Sykes slammed into the back of the trike. The jolt knocked Jenny out of the trike and onto the bonnet of Sykes's car. Sykes reached out to grab her.

"*HELP!*" she screamed.

Oliver leaped from the trike to help his friend. He landed on Sykes's arm and bit down hard. Sykes tossed the kitten into the back seat. The Dobermans lunged at him. Dodger jumped into the car, too. *"GRRRRR!"* He attacked the Dobermans. He knocked them back.

"Mr Fagin!" screamed Jenny. She was still clinging to the bonnet of the car. "Help!"

"I'm coming!" shouted Fagin.

Sykes grabbed at Jenny's leg. Fagin tugged at her arm.

The chase continued. The trike and the car sped out of the dark tunnel and onto a bridge. Ahead of them was a train. It was coming right towards them.

Fagin tugged harder. With one great heave he yanked Jenny back onto the trike. The train was about to hit them. Fagin swerved the trike sharply and ran it up the railing of the bridge. The train barrelled on. It crashed right into Sykes's car. The car exploded and plunged into the river below. The gang gasped. Dodger was in that car! And so was Oliver!

The gang rushed over to the railing of the bridge. Below, they could see only dark, churning water.

Behind them, Dodger stepped out of the shadows. In his mouth he held Oliver. The little kitten was limp and lifeless.

"Oliver!" Jenny screamed. "Please be all right!"

Oliver opened his eyes. He moved his mouth weakly.

"Mew," he said.

56

Jenny reached out and pulled the kitten to her. He was alive!

"Oh, Oliver!" Jenny cried.

18

Oliver went back to live with Jenny, and the gang returned with Fagin to their barge. They all remained great friends, though. They'd been through a lot together.

The day after their great escape was another special day, Jenny's birthday. Winston gave her a big party. They invited all the gang. Even Fagin came. The gang brought presents for their new friend—a broken watch, a chewed-up wallet. It was their usual assortment of junk.

"Thank you," Jenny said politely. Now it was time for cake.

"Don't forget to make a wish, Jenny," said Fagin.

Jenny looked fondly at Oliver.

"I know what I'll wish for," she said.

While Jenny cut the cake, Tito got up to show Georgette how to dance. Winston and Fagin wandered off together to watch TV. The telephone rang. It was Jenny's parents.

"You're at the airport?" Winston beamed. "She'll be so surprised to see you both. Right! I won't say a word."

"Well, we'd better be going," said Fagin. "Come on, you guys. The streets are calling. Let's go."

The dogs barked and ran to the trike. Winston put his arm around Fagin. Jenny kissed the old man goodbye.

"Well," Winston smiled at Fagin. "Thanks for everything."

Dodger was the last to leave. He wanted to say a special goodbye to Oliver.

"Hey, listen, kid," he said. "You take care of yourself. If you ever need anything or just want to hang out or anything, you know where to find me."

"Absitively. Posolutely," Oliver laughed.

With a last wink and a wag of his tail, Dodger took off after the trike.

Winston smiled as he watched Fagin depart.

"What a delightful scoundrel," he said.

Jenny and Oliver waved goodbye to their friends. The gang drove off into traffic. They were headed home, through the crazy, crowded streets of busy, bustling New York.